D0718836

Dennis
2a Cra
Glasg
Phor

This boo
be renev
date, aut

By Appointment to

Her Majesty
The Horrible Princess

Purveyors of Exceptional Yarns
and Rip-Roaring Adventures

Please enjoy this book with a cup
of afternoon tea in your finest china

With all love to
Oscar, Conrad, Caspar and the children
of Toad Avenue Primary School
A.M.

For my niece Georgia,
The Actually Very Lovely Princess

A T S

GLASGOW CITY COUNCIL	
LIBRARIES INFORMATION & LEARNING	
C004688782	
WITH	PETERS
07-Feb-2011	£5.99
JF	

First published in 2010
by Meadowside Children's Books
185 Fleet Street, London EC4A 2HS
www.meadowsidebooks.com

Text © Anna Maxted 2010
Illustrations © Alex T. Smith 2010

The rights of Anna Maxted and Alex T. Smith
to be identified as the author and illustrator
of this work have been asserted by them
in accordance with the Copyright,
Designs and Patents Act, 1988

Tom & Matt
THE
HORRIBLE
PRINCESS

Written by
ANNA MAXTED

Illustrated by
ALEX T. SMITH

meadowside
CHILDREN'S BOOKS

CONTENTS

1. Water Fight!

Tom and Matt were in the bathroom making a magic potion in a bucket.

"A slug of green slime!" said Matt, squeezing Mummy's shampoo out of the bottle.

"A blob of blue spit," sang Tom, squirting in Daddy's shaving foam until the tube was empty.

"A lump of old porridge," said Matt, dumping in Mummy's bath scrub.

"And a big fat squishy mint-flavoured worm," said Tom, squeezing in Daddy's toothpaste and stirring.

The bathroom door burst open and a bossy little voice said, **"I'M TELLING!"**

TOM & MATT

It was Isabella. Isabella lived across the road and Isabella's Mummy, Victoria, thought the children should be friends. Isabella liked to pretend she was a princess and that Tom and Matt were her servants. She would throw her dirty socks on the floor and say, 'Servants! Pick up my socks!'

As Tom and Matt did not even like to pick up their own dirty socks, this was not a game they enjoyed. Tom and Matt and Isabella were not friends. Only the Baby liked to play with Isabella.

"Please don't tell, Isasmella!" said Matt.

"I'm telling," said Isabella, "and it serves you right for calling me Isasmella!"

"NO!" hissed Tom, but it was too late. Isabella ran downstairs, and two seconds later,

Mummy thundered up the stairs like a lady elephant and appeared at the bathroom door. "Tom! Matt!" she gasped. "I don't believe this! You've wasted about **A MILLION POUNDS** worth of shampoo!"

"But this is a magic potion, Mummy," said Matt. "It's a cure for furry toes!"

Daddy's feet

"I don't have furry toes," growled Mummy. "But I do need to wash my hair!"

"Daddy has furry toes," said Tom.

"Yes, but he doesn't mind!" boomed Mummy. "Men love having furry toes! When you grow up, you'll have furry toes!"

"HA HAR!" said Isabella.

"I don't want furry toes!" wailed Matt. "I need the potion!"

Mummy made a face like a gorilla.

9

"Take a deep breath and count to ten, Mummy," said Tom.

Mummy sighed. "Play nicely," she said. "And please include Isabella!" Then she stamped downstairs to drink even more coffee with Isabella's Mummy, Victoria.

Tom and Matt decided to play Knights and Princesses and include Isabella. Daddy had made them cardboard shields and drawn a picture of a fighting dragon on the front of each. Tom and Matt tiptoed down to the kitchen and took two rolls of tin foil out of the drawer. They unrolled the foil into two beautiful long silver carpets, and used the cardboard tubes as swords. Their plastic swords had been taken away after the Baby had nearly received a poke in the eye.

Tom was the best swordsman in the world, and Matt was the best swordsman in history.

THE HORRIBLE PRINCESS

For extra protection, Tom and Matt filled their water pistols with cold water. Then, they crept down the hall. Isabella was playing tea parties with the Baby in his room and trying to get some sense out of him. As Baby was not quite three, getting sense out of him was hard work.

"Would you like a biscuit, Baby?" said Isabella.

"Look! I stand on my head!"

"Do you take milk and sugar, Baby?"

"I do wee on carpet!"

Tom whispered to Matt, "There's the Horrible Princess! She's kidnapped Baby and Tiny Dragon!"

Isabella looked up and said, "I know you're spying on me, Tom and Matt. And you don't even look like knights. You're wearing pirate trousers!"

This was true. Mummy and Daddy couldn't buy every costume in the world, even when it was your birthday, and the boys had chosen pirate outfits. Now Tom wished they had chosen knight outfits.

Then Isabella screamed, "Baby's doing a wee on the carpet!"

"ATTACK!" said Tom, and he burst in and squirted Isabella with his water pistol. Matt aimed too low and squirted Tiny Dragon. Sometimes, Tom and Matt knew they were going to get into trouble, but when you are having so much fun now, it is hard to care about later...

2. THE KIDNAPPED DRAGON

um... help?

Isabella grabbed Tom's water pistol and threw it on the floor. Then she ran downstairs crying, "Mummy, Mummy, they've ruined my princess dress!"

Tom and Matt's Mummy roared as loud as a lion with a thorn in its bottom, "Tom! Matt! Get down here!"

Then she said, "WHY did you squirt Isabella in the face with a water pistol?"

"I thought she was thirsty," said Matt.

"We were including her," said Tom.

Now, Mummy was in a cross mood. It was the hairdresser's fault. The hairdresser had coloured some of Mummy's hair golden and

SPOT THE DIFFERENCE	
GRUMPY MUMMY	GRUMPY GINGER CAT

some of it brown and when Isabella's Mummy, Victoria, saw the hairdo she said to Mummy, "Oh darling, you look like a ginger cat!" Victoria was not tactful.

'Tactful' means lying your head off, so you don't hurt peoples' feelings. For example, when Mummy asked Tom if he liked her hairdo, Tom – who was a kind boy – had tactfully replied, "I think it's so-so."

Matt was not tactful. He said, "Mummy, you look like that monster with bolts in his neck!"

Yes, Mummy was in a cross mood. And now, Victoria was annoyed with Mummy which made Mummy feel even crosser. Victoria said, "Isabella's dress is soaked! We'll have to go home!"

Then Baby slid downstairs, naked. He had coloured himself mostly orange with a felt tip and he was clutching Tiny Dragon. "Don't be sad!" he said to Isabella. "Have this dragon!"

Isabella snatched the dragon.

"That's my dragon!" said Matt.

"You must learn to share, Matt," said Victoria. "Isabella will give him back next time."

Isabella pressed her finger to her nose and made a face like a pig squashed against a window. Then she skipped out of the door, holding Tiny Dragon.

Matt was purple in the face and tears were flying out of his eyes – like when a dog shakes himself after a bath.

He shouted at Mummy, "Why did you let her take Tiny Dragon? He's my friend!"

"Look, I'm sorry," said Mummy, in a mean voice. "He's a stuffed toy. Now stop crying and go to your room and stay there!"

The truth was, Mummy felt as rotten as a 100-year old egg. She felt like a terrible Mummy for letting Isabella take Tiny Dragon. It hurt her heart to see Matt so sad. But she hadn't wanted to be rude to her guests – even when they were rude. It's hard for Mummies – they are almost perfect but not quite and sometimes they make **A BIG PARPING RASPBERRY** of a mistake.

"I like you, Mummy," sobbed Matt. "I just don't like your behaviour!"

"Don't worry," said Tom, putting his arm around Matt. "We'll rescue Tiny Dragon! We are knights in pirate trousers, so we are extra good at fighting! I am **SIR GALLOP HEAD**, and you are **SIR POPOFFALOT**. This is our first quest!"

Sir Gallophead

Sir Popoffalot

Pirate Trousers

3. The Quest is DOOMED

Tom and Matt ran to the Hideout to plan their quest. The Hideout was made out of chairs and blankets and when you went inside it made you invisible. But Matt was too sad about Isabella taking Tiny Dragon to plan the quest or become invisible.

Tiny Dragon was a soft dragon with purple wings that Matt slept with. Matt also slept with Mrs Dragon, Flat Ted, Lion, Bear, Rolly Dog and Renard (pronounced Rrrrrenaaarrrrrd – he was a French fox who was obsessed with chicken).

It was a slight squash in Matt's bed, but Mummy allowed it.

Mummy allowed Matt to sleep with the light on and wear a Spiderman suit instead of pyjamas. Mummy allowed Matt to drink milk from a bottle after brushing his teeth, and she would probably have allowed him to hang from his bunk bed ceiling and sleep upside down like a bat – as long as Matt spent the night in his own bed.

You see, when Matt was little he had come and slept in Mummy and Daddy's bed every night for a year. That's 365 nights during which Mummy and Daddy lay awake with cotton wool stuffed in their ears, and listened to Matt snore. He also had sharp toenails and rolled around in his sleep kicking people like footballs. As long as Matt spent the night not in Mummy's bed, she let him do whatever he liked.

"I can't sleep without Tiny Dragon!" said Matt. A second later, Matt fell asleep in the Hideout.

Tom lay down and tried to think of a plan to rescue Tiny Dragon.

"Can I play?" said Baby, poking his head into the Hideout. Baby saw that Matt was asleep. "I go to sleep!" he said, and climbed over Tom's head. This involved a smelly nappy in the face. Tom didn't say, 'Get your smelly nappy out of my face!' He just let Baby climb over his head. Tom was patient with Baby because Baby loved Tom. When Mummy cut Tom's toenails, Baby shouted, 'Don't hurt my boy!'

And Baby loved Matt. When Mummy cut Matt's toenails, Baby shouted, 'Don't hurt my friend!'

Because of Baby, Mummy was forced to cut Tom and Matt's toenails in the dead of night.

Baby snuggled his chubby little body next to Matt and fell asleep with his mouth open.

THE HORRIBLE PRINCESS

Tom sighed. Even though his two brothers could be annoying in the extreme – that's 11 out of 10 and a gold star in Being Annoying – they were fun. Now he had no one to discuss his plan with. In fact, there was no plan.

As Tom lay down to rest his eyes, he felt sad. How could he be a brave knight, who rescued tiny dragons from horrible princesses when he had to stay in his room? He didn't have a powerful steed (which is an old-fashioned word for a big horse that knights used to ride), he didn't even have a donkey. And the cat was far too small to ride on. He didn't dare tell Matt, but Tom worried that Tiny Dragon was **LOST FOREVER**.

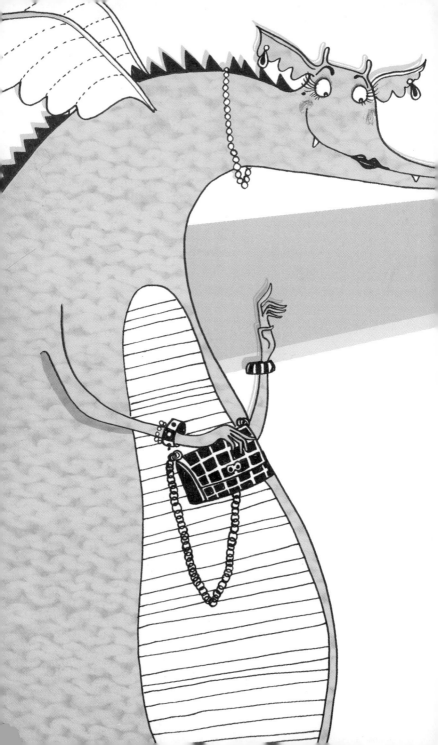

4. MUMMY TO THE RESCUE!

Matt was dreaming that Mummy was washing his face.

"Stop it!" he said, twisting away.

The flannel she was using was rough and smelled fishy.

Matt thought it must be the cat, giving him a wash. "Get off!" he said, pushing her away. Matt was very gentle with the cat and often when he stroked her, she licked him on the forehead as if he were a bald kitten.

"Yuck!" said Matt. He opened his eyes and saw that he was nose to snout with a massive dragon. "Help!" he yelled. "Please don't eat me!"

"Of course I'm not going to eat you," snapped the dragon. "You taste disgusting! When did you last wash your face? I'm trying to wake you up and I don't have an alarm clock!"

Tom woke to find that he couldn't move. This was because he was trapped beneath the large stomach of an enormous dragon.

"Do you mind?" said the dragon, her wings flapping against the ceiling of the Hideout.

"Your head appears to be wedged in my belly button."

The Hideout seemed to have grown to the size of a cave – but the dragon was so big she was still hogging all the space.

"Who are you?" squeaked Tom. "What do you want?" He wriggled out from under the dragon and grabbed his water pistol. "Don't even take a nibble of the baby's ear or I'll squirt you!"

"It's Mrs Dragon!" shouted Matt. "She sleeps with me in my bed! She's got all big and come alive!"

Tom looked more closely at Mrs Dragon. Matt was right. Mrs Dragon might be the size of a lorry, with sharp shiny claws, and smooth green scales, and great webbed purple wings – and she was breathing hot little puffs of smoke, and her long spiky tail was swishing crossly like a cat's – but he could still see the label above her left hind leg which said:

WASH AT 30 DEGREES

"You're Matt's toy," he said in surprise.

"I am Tiny Dragon's mother!" roared Mrs Dragon. A flame flickered out of her nostril and set the ceiling on fire. "And that Horrible Princess has kidnapped my little girl!"

Tom tactfully put out the fire with his water pistol without saying a word.

"Tiny Dragon is a girl?"

Mrs Dragon nodded and wiped away a tear. "She's his age." Mrs Dragon pointed a claw at the Baby, who was still asleep and drooling with his mouth open. "We have to rescue her now. We must all go to the Castle."

"The Castle?" said Tom. "What castle?"

"Isasmella doesn't live in a castle!" said Matt.

THE HORRIBLE PRINCESS

"My dears," said Mrs Dragon. "The Horrible Princess lives in a castle in The Kingdom of the Fairy Garden and that is where she has taken my dragon cub. I am putting together a team. And I understand that you are **FEARLESS KNIGHTS**, and he" – she jabbed at the Baby with a claw – "is a Fire Fighter."

The Baby was indeed under the mistaken impression that he worked for the Emergency Services.

He spent most of his day wearing a yellow helmet, pointing a hose and crushing peoples' feet under the wheels of his remarkably heavy ride-on fire engine.

"We are **FEARLESS KNIGHTS**," said Tom. "And Baby is a **ROGUE FIREMAN**."

A 'rogue' means 'a person who thinks he's brilliant at a job but is secretly rubbish.'

"But," Tom added sadly, "we're not allowed out of the house."

"I should think not!" said Mrs Dragon. "You're only nippers! But you would be travelling with me, a responsible adult!"

Tom glanced at the burnt ceiling.

"But we don't know the way to the Kingdom of the Fairy Garden," said Matt. "And I don't like the Under Growl. The trains smell of soot."

"We're not going on the Underground," said Mrs Dragon.

"Then how will we get there?" said Matt.

"We will fly of course!" said Mrs Dragon. "You three boys jump on my back. The Baby can sit in Tiny Dragon's child seat."

Tom gasped with excitement and Matt

jumped around and said: "Oh fank you, Mrs Dragon! I love you!"

Mrs Dragon turned pink. "Thank you, Sir Popoffalot. But I must warn you, this is a dangerous quest. We will be flying at a non-pressurised altitude of 3,000 feet. That's as high as a helicopter. Any fidgeting and you'll fall to the ground and go **SPLAT** like a squished tomato."

Tom gasped again – this time with worry. "Mrs Dragon," he said. "I think the quest is too dangerous for Baby."

What Tom meant was Baby was too dangerous for the quest. The Baby was, frankly ('frankly' means telling the bald truth), a loon from Planet Nutcase. His favourite game was jumping on the top bunk with a woolly hat pulled down over his eyes. That's about five different kinds of

DANGEROUS.

TOM & MATT

He ate food off the floor right by the cat's bowl. He loved to jump off anything high, and Tom thought that might include flying dragons.

"I'm sorry," said Tom, "but we need to leave the Fireman at home."

5. Catching the KNIGHT FLIGHT

DESTINATION:
KINGDOM OF THE
FAIRY GARDEN

FLIGHT NO.
DR007

SEAT NUMBER
0 0 1

DRAGON AIR
BOARDING CARD

Then Baby woke up and said, "Where the Christmas tree gone?"

The Baby often woke up and said stuff like: 'Archie burst my balloon.' Or: 'Mummy, why did you run off?' or: 'Where the Christmas tree gone?'

This was because once, about six months earlier, a dog called Archie had bitten his balloon and burst it. Well. Imagine if a friend in the park suddenly popped your football with a fork. What a nasty shock! You'd never forget it!

And, in January, the Christmas tree had indeed, gone. Baby couldn't understand it!

33

Happily, Mummy hadn't run off – Baby had dreamt that one. But he didn't know what a dream was – he thought that dreams were real and that life was a dream.

So now, waking up to a jumbo-sized dragon sitting at his feet, Baby just smiled and said, "Hello Mrs Dragon, you got big nose."

"What's all that shouting?" shouted Daddy from downstairs. "Is Baby on the top bunk?"

"No, Daddy!" shouted Tom. "Play nicely and include the Baby!" shouted Mummy from downstairs.

"Yes, Mummy!" shouted Matt.

As the people Next Door would agree, Tom and Matt came from a very shouty family.

Tom and Matt exchanged glances. Tom said: "Be-be, do you want to come wiv us to fight pwincess?"

THE HORRIBLE PRINCESS

Sorry about the spelling back there. You see, Tom spoke to Baby in a baby voice – even in front of his friends. This was quite brave as Tom's friends might have laughed at him. But they didn't – because Tom's friends spoke to their own little brothers or sisters in baby voices. Not always, but sometimes, as they knew it was comforting for the little ones. What kind children!

"Yeeeeaaaaaahhhh!" growled Baby, who didn't speak in a baby voice – he sounded more like a 40-year old tough guy. "I hit princess with stick! I smack her bot!"

Baby was very excited and packed a nappy in his backpack. He also packed his Grabber (a claw on a stick, which you squeezed to make the claw grab things). Then he packed his hose, and his fireman's helmet.

TOM & MATT

Tom grabbed his sword, a bottle of the magic potion and three pairs of pants. He took all his 'rubbish' – which is another word for 'sweets.' He also packed a bottle of milk for the Fireman – and bread and peanut butter. Mummy said that vegetables made you super-strong immediately, so he packed a carrot for emergencies.

Matt put on his green swimming goggles. He stuck his water pistol and his sword in the leg hole of his pants. He took his torch and Daddy's dressing gown belt. He also took the remote control because Daddy watched too much television.

"This is the final call to passengers for the **KNIGHT FLIGHT TO THE KINGDOM OF THE FAIRY GARDEN**," bellowed Mrs Dragon, who could never understand why it took small children so long to get ready.

THE HORRIBLE PRINCESS

"Prepare for take off!"

Tom grabbed the Baby by the scruff of the neck, scrambled up Mrs Dragon's tail, and plopped Baby in the child seat. "I do it! I do it!" shouted Baby – who liked to sit clacking vainly at his seatbelt till the seas ran dry and Mummy made a noise like a dog howling at the moon.

"Hurry, Matt!" shouted Tom, as Mrs Dragon flapped her great wings. Matt hurled Daddy's dressing gown cord and Tom caught the end of it. He pulled Matt up as Mrs Dragon launched into the air. Matt held on squealing. The boys clung to each other and squeezed their eyes shut. The wind rushed by in a whoosh, and they shot up, fast and high, as if they had been pinged into the air from a catapult.

6

Marshmallow clouds

"Snakes alive!" shouted Matt. "We're going to bash through the roof!"

But their house, the roof, the walls and the door seemed to melt away – and moments later they were soaring through the wide blue sky, with the air smelling of blossom and fresh cut grass, and the sun's rays warm on their skin. "Look, Tom!" cried Matt. "The world is made of toys!"

Tom peered over the edge of Mrs Dragon's wing – far, far below, all the houses and cars were tiny – and when he looked up, the clouds were near enough to touch; they looked like marshmallow. He reached out and pulled a tuft; it was marshmallow!

"Matt! Baby!" he said, grabbing handfuls as they flapped past, "have some of this!"

"Faster! Faster!" shouted Baby. **"LIKE RACING CAR!"**

"Don't eat too much cloud!" barked Mrs Dragon over her shoulder. "Your teeth will turn lemon yellow and fall out!"

Matt's worst thing was being told off – even for really bad things like trying to seal the Baby in an envelope. His other worst thing was grown-ups who spoke in a rude, cross way to children then went bananas if children spoke in a rude, cross way to them.

But Matt saw that Mrs Dragon was worried about Tiny Dragon. So all he said was: "I don't think I heard a please!"

Then he said "Look!" but because he'd forgotten about not talking with your mouth full, he actually said "Gak!" and nearly choked on a piece of marshmallow. "Over there! The whole thing is pink!"

TOM & MATT

Tom looked. Far below was a patchwork land of fields and forests, farms and cottages, mountains and caves, rivers and lakes, and, high on a hill, one great glittery glass castle, with turrets and towers, and arrow-slit windows and a moat and a drawbridge. All the buildings were pink.

"**IT'S BEAUTIFUL!**" said Baby.

"**PINK STINKS!**" said Tom.

Mrs Dragon swooped low until they were just above the trees. Then she dived sharply down and skidded to a halt in a pile of leaves, just outside the castle walls.

THE HORRIBLE PRINCESS

It was lucky that Tom and Matt were wearing seatbelts or they would have flown right over her head and gone crunch into a tree.

"QUIET PLEASE!" said Mrs Dragon, unclipping the Baby. "If we want to succeed in our quest we have to listen and focus and – young man, stop picking your nose!

"We have a great challenge ahead," said Mrs Dragon, "so does anyone need to go to the toilet?"

Matt started to hop on the spot.

"He doesn't like to go in front of people, or dragons," explained Tom.

"Not a problem!" said Mrs Dragon. The boys watched as Mrs Dragon started to dig furiously with her front paws. In one minute, she had scooped out a hole that you could drop a house into. Everyone turned their back while Matt scrambled into it and did an underground wee.

"Now wash your hands!" said Mrs Dragon. "I've got baby wipes, or dragon spit, which would you prefer?"

"WIPES!" yelled Matt. "I prefer wipes!"

"No need to shout," said Mrs Dragon. "Now, listen up! The Horrible Princess always wants what other children have got. If you had a booger in a tissue, she'd want it! If she thinks we want Tiny Dragon, she won't give her back. We are going to have to sneak into the Castle and steal back Tiny Dragon without being seen. Luckily, I know a spell to make us invisible!"

7. The Invisibility Spell

Mrs Dragon waved her paw like a wand and said: "A red bus, a blue bus, now they can't see us!

"BOOM!" added Mrs Dragon. "There we go!"

"Um, Mrs Dragon," said Tom.

"What is it?"

"I can still see you... and Matt... and Baby."

Mrs Dragon sighed. "Tom. Of course we can see us – otherwise we'd bump into each other. But they – the enemy – can't see us! Not so much as a whisker or a claw or a nappied bottom!"

"Okay," said Tom, gazing at Mrs Dragon, who was the size of a tyrannosaurus and bright green, "if you're sure."

"I'm certain," said Mrs Dragon, briskly. "And now, off to the castle we go!"

8. Kissing Frogs
(and Eating Food off the floor)

The Baby spat a leaf out of his mouth. Then he said "Yummy!" and put it back in again.

"No, Baby!" said Tom. **"POISON!"**

Mrs Dragon said, "In the Kingdom of the Fairy Garden, sweets grow on trees. Even the dog pooh is made of chocolate."

"I'm still not eating it," said Tom. "No way."

PHOO!

TOM & MATT

Tom was sensible about only eating food from his plate. This was because Daddy had told him that when Daddy first met Mummy and they had cats instead of children, Daddy had seen **A CRUMB OF CHOCOLATE** on the floor. Instead of getting out the dustpan and brush, Daddy thought it would be a good idea to eat that crumb of chocolate from the floor. Sadly, it turned out not to be chocolate. It was a **SMALL PIECE OF CAT POOH**, attached to a crumb of cat litter. The cat had shaken it off his paw.

Whenever Tom saw food on the floor, even if it looked delicious, he wouldn't touch it. But the Baby, I'm sorry to say, saw no difference between Daddy's lovingly-prepared

spaghetti Bolognese, and other disgusting unmentionables. An 'unmentionable' is something so yucky that you don't even want to mention it.

Sorry, where were we? Ah yes. The boys and Mrs Dragon were tiptoeing towards the Castle.

Tom looked through his binoculars to see if he could spot any soldiers guarding the castle. Then he heard a croaking sound.

"HELP!" said Baby, clinging to Tom's leg like a koala. "That frog is going to eat me!"

Tom looked at the road. There were hundreds of frogs, hopping in all directions.

TOM & MATT

"Hello, Charles, Robert, William, Jim, Henry and Rupert!" said Mrs Dragon, waving at the frogs. "The Queen grows frogspawn in the Castle moat. The frogs are taken to **TOAD AVENUE PRIMARY SCHOOL** and every day before assembly all the little girls in years 2, 3, 4, and 5 have to **KISS THE FROGS**."

"Ugh!" said Tom. "That's disgusting! Why?"

"In the hope that one frog will change into a **HANDSOME PRINCE** and play with the Horrible Princess. But they never do change. They prefer being frogs."

"But," said Tom, "a frog must be kissed by a princess to change into a prince."

"My dear," said Mrs Dragon. "Every little girl is a princess, just as every little boy is a prince and every baby is beautiful even if it's a purple moon-faced screamer. Now, quiet! We're getting close to the castle!"

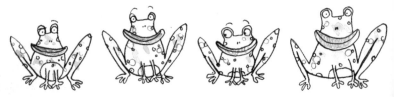

9. LITTLE MONKEY

"How are we going to get in?" said Matt.

"We can fly up to the battlements," said Mrs Dragon. "And sneak in from there."

The boys jumped on, and Mrs Dragon flapped into the sky.

Tom was trying to see over the curve of the horizon when a pebble hit his ear.

"Ow!" he said. "Ow! Ow! Ow!"

They were under attack!

Tom caught one of the pebbles. It wasn't a pebble; it was a pink round sweet – like a lollipop not on a stick.

51

All over the place, pink round sweets were flying at them like stones.

"It's the Toy Army!" shouted Mrs Dragon. "The Princess has trained all her dolls to fight like ninjas! They spend all morning trying on dresses and all afternoon doing high kicks and shouting 'hi-ya!'."

"Yum," said the Baby, stuffing a sweet in his mouth, even though he wasn't allowed them. "I like this one!"

Mrs Dragon shouted, **"DON'T EAT THE SWEETS! THEY'LL TURN YOU INTO A MONKEY!"**

"How can the dolls see us?" said Tom. "I thought you chanted a spell to make us invisible!"

"Pardon, Mrs Dragon?" said Matt. "What was that you said about the sweets?

They turn you into a wh.. agh! The Baby's turned into **A MONKEY**!"

Mrs Dragon wasn't listening. She was talking to herself. "I did chant a spell!" she muttered, shaking her head. "I can't understand why it didn't work! I said 'Red bus, Blue bus, now you can't see us!' – oh dear – I think I got the spell mixed up with a nursery rhyme."

"What are we going to do, Mrs Dragon?" yelled Tom. "The Baby's turned into an ape! How can we change him back?"

The Baby jumped up and down on Mrs Dragon's back and said, "Oo-oo-oo!"

Mrs Dragon looked at Baby. "Oh," she said. "Baby has changed into a teenager!"

"No," said Tom. "A monkey!"

"Ah yes," agreed Mrs Dragon. "But Baby is so much cuter as a monkey! I've got no idea how to change him back! Don't worry – I'm sure your Mummy won't mind!"

She landed on the castle roof with a thump. The dolls sped towards them. They all had yellow hair, wore pink dresses and roller skates. They all carried blasters that shot out pink sweets – and even though the dolls only came up to Matt's knee, they were horribly spooky, like sad clowns.

"Quick," said Tom. "Mrs Dragon, try and distract them."

As Tom, Matt and the Monkey ran for cover, Mrs Dragon started jumping about like a monster kangaroo. All the dolls were so busy staring that they forgot to shoot their blasters.

"What is Mrs Dragon doing?" said Tom.

"I fink she doing exercise," said Baby. Except no one understood him because he said it in monkey language which was, "Oo-oo-oo!"

"She's dancing!" said Matt. "She's doing ballet!" Then he wailed, "I don't want a monkey for a brother!"

"I'm not sure I can tell the difference!" said Tom. "Run down these stairs! Quick!"

10 THE POTION FOR... FURRY TOES

The stairs went round and round like if you peel an apple in one long curl. Finally, they stopped and there was floor.

"This room is **GIANT**," said Matt.

"It's the **BANQUETING HALL**," said Tom.

"The **BED-WETTING HALL**?" said Matt.

"No, **IDIOT**," said Tom, "the hall where you eat!"

Oh dear. I don't know about you, but in Tom and Matt's house, when someone calls someone else a you-know-what it starts a fight that lasts as long as a maths lesson.

"I'm not an **IDIOT**!" said Matt. "**YOU'RE** an **IDIOT**!"

"I know you are," said Tom, "but what am I?"

"You're an **IDIOT**," said Matt, and **WHACKED HIM ON THE HEAD** with his cardboard-tube sword.

"I know you are," said Tom, grabbing Matt by the neck and shaking him like a maraca. "But what am I?"

"YOU'RE THE WORST BROTHER IN THE WORLD," screamed Matt, trying to bite Tom's arm. **"WORSE THAN A MONKEY!"**

Suddenly, Matt unclamped his teeth from Tom's arm and said, "I got an idea! Where's the potion for furry toes?"

"In my backpack," said Tom. "Why?"

"I need it," said Matt. Tom gave him the bottle, and Matt poured some onto a spoon. "Drink it!" he said to the Monkey.

TOM & MATT

"You'll poison him!" said Tom. "It's made of shampoo!"

"Not here," said Matt. "Here it's magic!"

"But he's already got furry toes! He's got furry feet, furry arms, furry legs and a furry bottom!"

"Exactly!" said Matt. "So the spell should work backwards!"

As the Monkey swallowed the potion, Tom closed his eyes. He was scared to open them, just in case the spell worked double instead of backwards and Baby was no longer a monkey but a woolly mammoth.

11. Pidiots and NITWITS

"Pidiots!" said the Baby, and pinched Tom on the bottom with his Grabber.

"Hooray!" shouted Tom. **"IT WORKED! MATT, YOU'RE A GENIUS!"**

Tom was so pleased to have Baby back that he didn't even mind being called a Pidiot.

Normally, when the Baby called his brothers 'Pidiot' – a cross between 'Pooh' and 'Idiot' – one of them would give him a smack. Yes, that's right, even though Mummy and Daddy said every single day, 'You are not allowed to hit,' sometimes, the boys got so cross that it was very hard not to hit.

Daddy's new rule was that if you wanted to

GLUE

hit, you had to stick your hands in your pockets and pretend they were glued there. Then you called Daddy or Mummy and they would sort it out. If you kept your patience, you got to do something fun like have a spooky bath (when Mummy made the water green, put on a witch's hat, and stirred them, like in a cauldron). If you did hit, there would be lots of crying and shouting and zero fun. Hm. Probably better not to hit.

"LOOK!" squealed Baby. "Tiny Dragon and Princess!"

Tom quickly pulled his brothers into a dark corner to hide.

Isabella skipped into the banqueting hall, with Tiny Dragon waddling after her. Then she stuck a piece of pink cloud on a fork.

Princess Isabella held the fork in front of Tiny Dragon's nose. Tiny Dragon coughed.

"Come on," said Princess Isabella. **"BLOW!"**

And then Tiny Dragon huff-puffed and a little spurt of flame came out of her nose and toasted the cloud.

"Hooray!" said Isabella, and ate the marshmallow without even saying to Tiny Dragon, 'Do you want a bit?'

"How are we going to rescue Tiny Dragon?" whispered Matt.

"We'll have to stay super quiet and snatch her when the Horrible Princess goes to the toilet."

"When's she going to the toilet?"

"I don't know!" hissed Tom. "But everyone goes to the toilet – even princesses! So we must stay super quiet until then."

They watched as Isabella made Tiny Dragon breathe fire again.

"THAT'S DANGEROUS!" shouted Baby, running out and squirting Isabella with his Fireman's hose. Even though it was pretend and Baby was making the **'SHSSS! SSSHHH!'** noises of the water himself, this was a Fairy Kingdom, so a flood of water shot out and Isabella got soaked.

"No, Baby!" shouted Tom – and ran after him. Matt ran after Tom, even though he was scared.

Matt was still a little boy and cried if he had a nightmare or hurt his knee, but Matt had the heart of a lion. That means he was very brave. It is okay for boys to cry – it doesn't mean they're not brave. I know, because Matt cried a lot and he was very brave. Or, as Daddy said, he was 'as tough as old boots'.

"Dolls!" shouted Isabella. "Arrest them! And stick them in the dungeon – the one full of **CAKE, TOYS, FOOTBALLS, AND TELEVISION**!" Then she shouted, "Joke, ha ha! Put them in:

THE DEEPEST, DARKEST STINKIEST DUNGEON AND THROW AWAY THE KEY..."

The dolls marched Tom and Matt down slimy, slippery stone stairs, until they stood before a thick wooden door. One doll unlocked the door and pushed them into a cold, damp cellar. There were green puddles of smelly water on the floor, and Tom thought he saw a rat. There was one small window.

"Where's Baby?" said Tom. He felt sick suddenly.

"The Princess has decided to appoint the Baby Fire Fighter in Chief."

"But he's not even three!" said Tom. "He hasn't the foggiest idea how to fight fires! He could get seriously hurt! He just likes sliding down poles and climbing ladders! He doesn't even know that fire is hot!"

"He'll learn!" said the Doll, who didn't have very good listening skills. Then she slammed the door and locked it.

Matt said, "Where's the television?"

"There is no television!" said Tom. "The Horrible Princess said it for a mean joke."

He was frightened but he didn't call Matt a you-know-what, because he knew Matt was frightened too.

Matt said, "It's too dark. Turn on the light."

"There is no light," sighed Tom.

"I know!" said Matt. "I got my torch!" He pulled it out of his backpack, and switched it on. Now it was light, but now they could see that there was a big spider web in each corner, each with a big fat spider sitting in the middle.

"I don't like spiders," wailed Matt. "I want to see Baby!"

"Let's have a picnic," said Tom,

because he didn't
want Matt to cry. He was
also hungry. Tom made peanut butter
sandwiches. They had a few bites of
carrot, and he even shared his sweets.

It is hard to share something that is
your favourite, but Daddy had told Tom
that real knights had good manners. They
knew how to fight, and they were polite.
('I've chopped off your arm! I do apologise –
would you like a plaster?')

Tom shone the torch around the dungeon.
The window was too small to squeeze through.
He pushed against the door, but it was like
pushing against a tree. Tom tried to keep calm.
But it was hard because he was worried about
Baby. The Princess was such a you-know-what
that she would probably let Baby drive a real
fire engine.

They finished eating and Matt said, "Now
the spiders will eat us!"

"Don't worry, Matt," said Tom. "Mrs Dragon
will rescue us!"

Then Matt dropped his torch. The torch went out, and Matt couldn't see and trod in a puddle. "My foot is slimy and green and it stinks!" he wailed.

Usually, Matt liked to splash in every puddle and often returned from the park wet up to the neck, even in summer.

"Forget about your slimy green stinking foot, we need to let Mrs Dragon know where we are. Climb onto my shoulders and look out of that window."

Matt climbed on to Tom's shoulders.

"MRS DRAAAAGON!" called Matt in a deafening whisper. **"MRS DRAAAAGON! HELP US!"**

"Listen!" said Tom. "What's that sound?"

It was a flapping noise – Mrs Dragon was coming to the rescue!

13.

SHUSHUSHU FLUFLUFLU

"I see her!" shouted Matt. "There she is!"

He held onto the bars of the window and pulled himself up until he was standing on Tom's head.

"We're here, Mrs Dragon! We're in the stinky old dungeon!"

The other day, Daddy had been making himself a cheese sandwich and had accidentally trodden on the cat's paw. The cat had made a noise like this: **'YEEEEEOOOOAAAW!'** Now Matt screeched like the cat – a high, long, and hideous noise that made Tom's ears itch.

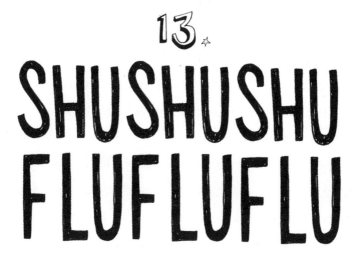

"What?" he yelled. "What's happened?"

Matt slithered down Tom's back, leaving a slime trail. He tried to say something but it came out as 'shushsushsushuflufluflufluflufluflu'

"What?" shouted Tom. **"WHAT IS IT?"**

But the more Tom shouted, the more Matt behaved like a hysterical jelly – he was crying and shaking and Tom couldn't understand a word.

Tom stopped shouting. He gave Matt a hug which was Matt's favourite thing. Even when Tom felt Matt wiping his nose on his top, he just kept hugging Matt until Matt felt better.

Then Tom said again, "What was it?"

"It was Mrs Dragon," said Matt. "She flew away."

14 ALL ALONE

"What!" shouted Tom. **"SHUSHUSHUFLU-FLUFLU?"**

"Yes!" said Matt. "She flew away! She flapped into the sky like a big green flying dragon!"

"She is a big green flying dragon!"

"Yes!" said Matt. "So that's exactly what she was like! She's gone home without us! Why? I thought she was our friend!"

Tom couldn't understand it. "Was Tiny Dragon on her back? Or Baby?"

"I don't know!" screeched Matt. "I couldn't see – she was too high up!"

Had Mrs Dragon rescued Tiny Dragon

but forgotten about them? Did she think they were big enough to get home by themselves? Tom had no idea how to get home.

"Now we're stuck in this dungeon," sobbed Matt, "and we'll never see Mummy and Daddy again!"

"Don't be silly," said Tom.

"I want my Mummy!" sobbed Matt. "I want my Daddy! I want my Baby!"

So do I, thought Tom. Sometimes, when Mummy wouldn't let him watch his programme, Tom felt like he hated Mummy. And sometimes, when Daddy told him off when it wasn't his fault, Tom felt like he hated Daddy. And sometimes, when Baby played with his toys and broke them, Tom felt like he hated Baby.

But mostly, he loved Mummy, because she drew pictures with him even though she was rubbish at drawing, and found things he had lost, and mostly, he loved Daddy because Daddy took him running in the park and

made Tom feel special and big, and mostly, he loved Baby, because Baby was funny and silly, and shouted 'talk to the book!' when he wanted to be read a story, and if Tom hurt himself, Baby stroked Tom's face with his soft little hands and said, 'Are you okay?'

Tom was more scared than he had ever been in his life.

"Matt," he said. "We will get out. We'll just have to find a way to escape by ourselves."

PANTS ON FIRE

"Gather your weapons," said Tom in a serious voice.

They looked for their swords and shields – but they had left them in the banqueting hall. Oh no! They didn't have any other supplies apart from Daddy's remote control and a lot of pants.

"I got my water pistol," said Matt, "but I got no water." His mouth started to turn downwards. "I haven't even got shiny armour! It's not fair!"

Tom didn't have shiny armour either. "It doesn't matter," he said, trying to explain. "Look, Matt. You are good at dancing, even when there is no music. And I am good at football, even when I am in the bath. We are brave knights – and so what if we are wearing pirate trousers? We are knights to the bone!"

Tom pulled Daddy's dressing gown belt out of Matt's backpack. "Sir Popoffalot – you have packed wisely and well!"

Tom whispered in Matt's ear. Carefully, Matt knelt on the dirty ground and filled his water pistol with the stinky green water.

Then the two boys started bashing the door with Tom's pants. Matt whispered, "Will it work, Tom?"

"Of course!" said Tom. He shouted,

"THE DOOR'S ON FIRE!

WE'RE PUTTING OUT THE FIRE WITH OUR PANTS!"

"Is this what real firemen do?" said Matt.

"Only if the hose runs out of water," said Tom.

TOM & MATT

There was a clinking of a key in the lock, and a big tough guy voice growled, "I do it!"

Hooray! The Fire fighter in Chief had come to put out the fire!

Tom and Matt gave each other a high five and Tom didn't say 'Down low' then pull his hand away and say 'Too slow!'

A bossy voice said, "Hurry up, Fire Chief! I don't want that door burning down! And I don't want those boys hitting it with their pants!" It was Princess Isabella.

Isabella's Mummy

Isabella's Mummy was a fussy, bossy sort of mummy who liked everything to be quiet and neat. Isabella wasn't allowed to shout or run, or talk in a silly voice, or wrestle, or paint her hands, or jump on the bed, or splash in the bath, or pick the label off a bottle, or try on grown-up shoes, or make chairs into a den, or hit a door with her knickers.

So when Isabella saw other children having

fun, she told them off. She didn't know that it was normal for children to act like zoo monkeys on occasion. 'On occasion' means 'for a short while and stopping before Mummy's head explodes.'

Matt and Tom's Mummy did let her children behave like zoo monkeys on occasion, every day. This was because she didn't like shouting all the time.

Princess Isabella burst in, with Baby right behind her. Baby was wearing his fireman's helmet, and holding his hose and his grabber, and he looked very important.

When he saw his brothers he shouted "Hi guys!" and ran to hug them.

"Put out the fire!" said Princess Isabella.

Then she added, "Where is the fire?"

Then Matt squirted her with his water pistol full of green slimy stinky water.

"Stop it!" she shouted. "This dress is made from gold sequins and silk! Why are you so mean to me?"

"Because you are mean to us!" shouted Matt. "You locked us in a dungeon! **YOU STARTED IT**!"

"NO, YOU STARTED IT!" said Isabella. "I wanted to play with you! But you wouldn't share your toys!"

"No, you started it! You told Mummy about the potion!" said Matt, who could go on like this for ever. Matt squirted slime on Isabella's beautiful dress, and Isabella burst into tears and ran out.

"That girl's my friend," said Baby.

"No she isn't, Baby! She's a baddie!" said Tom. Quickly, he grabbed the key from Isabella, slammed the door behind her, and locked it.

Matt stared at him in horror. "But now we are all prisoners! Baby too!"

16. THE REMOTE CONTROL

and the Cold Moat (Brr!)

"We are going to escape through that window and swim across the moat!" said Tom.

Matt scratched his head. "Tom," he said. "We can't fit through that window. Our heads are too big."

Tom waved Daddy's remote control. "Watch this!" he said.

"Programme!" shouted Baby. "I want my programme!"

"No programme!" hissed Tom. "Later!"

"I want my programme now!"

"NO BABY!" said Tom. "Television broken!"

"Awwwwwww!" said Baby, and collapsed on the floor, howling.

THE HORRIBLE PRINCESS

"Look, Baby!" said Tom. And he pressed the remote.

The small high window changed to a big high window.

Tom pressed the remote again.

The big high window changed to a big high door.

Tom pressed the remote again.

The big high door opened and there was a man in a builder's hat chatting to a yellow digger. "Programme!" yelled Baby.

"I hate that one!" moaned Matt.

Tom quickly pressed the remote again – but nothing happened. "Oh no," he gasped. "It's nearly out of batteries!"

He pressed and pressed – and just as he was about to give up, the man and the digger and the door vanished and there was a big window, just above the ground, perfect for climbing through.

"COME ON!" said Tom. "Let's jump before we're discovered!"

Baby and Matt shook their heads. "There might be sharks in that moat!" said Matt.

"And whales," said Baby.

"Matt," said Tom. "I am almost sixty seven per cent sure that there are no sharks in that moat."

"Ok, then," said Matt, who was only just starting to learn maths. "Let's jump! I can swim underwater. I can hold my breath for an hour."

I'm afraid this wasn't true. Matt thought he could hold his breath for an hour because when he went underwater and got Mummy to count the seconds, she counted extra fast. Now mummies do that sometimes – because they want their children to feel good about themselves. Daddies also want their children to feel good about themselves – and they do this by shouting 'Kick the ball HARDER! What's the MATTER with you, you big NUMBSKULL? Are your legs made of JELLY?'

"Don't want to go in the water!" said Baby. "That frog is going to eat me!"

"We'll help you swim, Baby," said Tom.

"READY, STEADY; JUMP!"

Baby sank like a brick, so Tom and Matt dived underwater, and pulled him to safety. He cried, "Don't like that jelly!" and spat out a mouthful of frogspawn.

Tom dragged Baby to the side of the moat, and they kicked their feet to stay afloat. But the sides were muddy, steep and too slippery to climb.

Then Tom spotted something pink in the mud. "Look!" he said. "It's one of those pink sweets. Eat it, Matt, and you'll change into a **MONKEY**. Then you can scamper up, hang on to the drawbridge with your tail, and pull us up with the dressing gown rope. Do it!"

Matt could sometimes be tricked into being helpful. Daddy might say, "Matt, could you pass me the phone – from upstairs?" or "Matt, could you hand me my slippers – from the bedroom?"

And mostly, Matt would say, "Yes, but I need you to come with me!" But once or twice he would kindly trudge upstairs and fetch Daddy's slippers while Daddy lay on the sofa. Matt was a very helpful boy. But there was no way he was going to agree to be changed into a **MONKEY**.

"No," said Matt. "Think of another plan."

"I can't," said Tom. Sometimes he got fed up of being the oldest and always having to look after the little ones. "I'm too tired! Baby is so heavy and wriggly – it's like trying to keep hold of a giant squid! We were stuck in the prison and now we're stuck in the moat! I'm cold and wet and I feel like giving up!"

17. Tiny Dragon does some Gardening

Just then, they heard a little cough.

Hang on... that cough... it sounded like...

"TINY DRAGON!" shouted Matt. "Look! She's still here!"

There, on the castle lawn, Princess Isabella was trying to make Tiny Dragon hold a cup of tea. When you have podgy little dragon claws, it's quite difficult to hold a cup – which is why dragons prefer to lap their tea out of bowls.

THE HORRIBLE PRINCESS

Matt began to mutter under his breath.

"What are you doing?" said Tom.

"Dragons have very good hearing," he said. "Like dogs!"

Suddenly, Tiny Dragon jumped up, and started to dig with her front paws.

"Stop it, Tiny!" shouted Isabella. "Please! You're ruining the grass! Stop! Come and have tea! I made you a chocolate cake!"

But Tiny Dragon kept digging. She dug and dug until she had dug a tunnel from the middle of the lawn to the edge of the moat. A hole appeared in the earth wall at the side of the moat. A little green snout poked out.

"THAT'S MY TINY DRAGON!" shouted Matt. Tiny Dragon leant forward and licked Matt on the nose.

Then she disappeared into the hole.

"Hooray," shouted Matt, as he, Tom, and Baby scrambled after her. The hole was big enough to crawl through, and Matt said, "I feel like a fox!"

They all popped up in the middle of the ruined lawn, and Tiny Dragon jumped into Matt's arms.

Princess Isabella stamped her foot. "But I was playing with her!"

"No!" said Matt. "It's my turn!"

"I know," said Baby. "We can share!"

The truth was that Baby liked other children to share their toys with him, but he did not like to share his toys with them, and if Mummy tried to make him, he fell to the floor and screeched till he was blue in the face. Still, it was a nice thing to say.

Tom and Matt and Princess Isabella looked at each other. "Fine," said Tom. "Fine," said Matt. "Fine," said Isabella, "but only if you say sorry!"

"Dorry!" said Matt.

"Dorry isn't sorry," said Isabella who knew that trick.

"I don't want to say sorry!" shouted Matt.

"Fine," said Isabella. "Dolls! Arrest them! Again!"

THE HORRIBLE PRINCESS

Hundreds of doll guards started to roller skate towards them from all directions. Tiny Dragon hid under Matt's jumper.

"**SIR POPOFFALOT** to the rescue!" shouted Matt. "Don't be scared Tiny Dragon! We'll protect you!"

When Matt said this, **SOMETHING MAGIC HAPPENED**. Matt and Tom felt tingly and when they looked down, they were wearing **SHINY SILVER SUITS OF ARMOUR** and helmets, and holding their swords! The dragon shields that Daddy had made appeared from nowhere and hovered in the air – Matt and Tom stared for a second then grabbed them. Meanwhile, the Baby found himself wearing a full fire fighter's uniform. It was a bit big.

"**PIDIOT!**" shouted Baby and clonked a guard on the head with his Grabber.

TOM & MATT

"**ON GUARD!**" said Matt, and trod hard on a guard's foot. "**ON ANOTHER GUARD!**" he said, and hit another guard on the knee.

Tom and Matt fought each other a lot at home. As I said, Tom was **THE BEST SWORDSMAN IN THE WORLD**, and Matt was **THE BEST SWORDSMAN IN HISTORY**. So they bravely fought off the dolls, 'Clang! Clang! Clang!' with their cardboard swords. Tom jumped and ducked to avoid being jabbed – the dolls had wands which were extremely poky. Matt rolled on the ground and tripped up one of the dolls with his foot.

"Ow!" he said. Princess Isabella had pulled his hair. Princess Isabella was a good fighter.

"We will defend Tiny Dragon to the death!" shouted Tom.

THE HORRIBLE PRINCESS

"We are **KNIGHTS OF THE REALM**!"

'Knights of the Realm' means 'Very important Royal knights.'

"Yes!" squeaked Matt. "We are **KNIGHTS OVERWHELMED**!"

'Knights Overwhelmed' means 'Knights in Big Trouble Because they are Surrounded by Soldiers.'

Matt had got his words mixed up... but he was right... they were Knights in Big Trouble.

19. Dragon ATTACK

There was a loud flapping noise in the sky, and such a powerful wind that Princess Isabella's pointy hat flew off her head and landed in the duck pond. A huge red dragon with angry red eyes landed on the lawn with a thump that shook the ground. It roared, as loud as an erupting volcano: "RAAAAAAAA AAAAAAAAAAAAAAAAAAAAAAH!" Fire and black smoke bellowed from its nostrils.

"That's DANGEROUS!" shouted Baby, and squirted out the fire with his hose.

"Baby," said Matt, "you are actually a very good fire fighter!"

Isabella scooped up Baby and hid under a chair. The dolls started to run, but the huge red dragon pinned each one of them to the ground with a claw at the back of their skirts. Tom and Matt stood still in terror. Was this a baddie dragon? Was it picnic time? Was he going to eat them for dinner, with Baby as dessert?

20 Mummies DON'T RUN OFF

"Daddy!" squeaked Tiny Dragon.

"Tallulah-Jane!" bellowed Daddy Dragon, sweeping up Tiny Dragon in his arms and throwing her high into the air then catching her like a beach ball. As he caught her he trod on Tom's foot. "Sorry Tom!" he growled. "Pardon me!"

"It's ok, Mr Dragon," said Tom, who felt wobbly with relief. He recognised Daddy Dragon now – he was a beautifully made red plastic dragon that Tom had got for his toy castle last Christmas.

"My little precious!" said Mrs Dragon, landing on Isabella's tea table and squashing the chocolate cake. She kissed Tiny Dragon, then she kissed Tom and Matt – and Baby.

"Yuck!" said Baby.

"You are my heroes!" said Mrs Dragon. **"YOU WERE SO BRAVE!"**

"You weren't brave!" said Matt, in a cross voice. "We were stuck in the dungeon and you flew off!"

"I'm sorry, Matt. I flew off to find Daddy Dragon – to help us rescue Tiny from the Horrible Princess."

"Stop calling me that!" shouted Isabella from under the chair. Tom saw that she was holding Baby's hand. "I just wanted a friend! I made Tiny Dragon a **CHOCOLATE CAKE** and then we were going to play hide and seek!"

Mrs Dragon's tail twitched. It was covered in chocolate cake from when she'd landed on the tea table and everyone got splattered.

"Yum," said Daddy Dragon, licking cake off his nose. He lifted the chair off Isabella.

"Don't hurt her!" shouted Tom. Even though Isabella was not his favourite, he did not want to see her toasted like a marshmallow. And she was kind to Baby.

"I don't toast children!" snapped Daddy Dragon. "I toast bread and occasionally croissants!" He cleared his throat. "Now, Isabella," he said in a gentle voice. "I know you wanted a friend, but we don't take dragons that belong to other people, do we? By the way, could you give me the recipe for that cake?"

"No. Yes," said Isabella. "I'm sorry." She looked sad. Then Baby started wriggling and shouting "Stop tickling me!"

Just as Tom began to wonder if Baby was actually bonkers, a frog jumped out of Baby's top. It had got stuck in there from the moat.

FROG Prince

"Oh, it's Henry!" said Mrs Dragon to Isabella. "He's a delightful young man! **KISS HIM**!"

Isabella shook her head. "I couldn't kiss a frog!" she said.

"Imagine that you are kissing a friend hello," said Mrs Dragon.

Then she called, **"ALL ABOARD FOR THE KNIGHT FLIGHT!"** Tom and Matt and Baby scrambled on to her back. Tiny Dragon jumped on to Daddy Dragon's back, and soon, they were soaring high, high in the blue sky.

And when Tom looked back, he saw Isabella, and with her was a tall, kind-looking boy, with muddy trousers. He looked as though he would be fun to play with, good at hide and seek and climbing trees. He had already taken off his crown and used it as a Frisbee.

22. Brave Knights and Fair Princesses

Tom and Matt and Baby woke up in the Hideout. Daddy had his head in a cupboard and was shouting, "Where do we keep the toilet paper?"

Matt jumped up. "We are knights, Daddy! Look at our armour! OH!"

The boys gazed at each other in disappointment. They were back in their pirate trousers.

"Mm-hmm," said Daddy, who was thinking about dinner – he wanted pizza but Mummy wanted salmon. This meant that Daddy would be eating salmon for dinner.

"We fought all the guards with our swords!"

said Tom. "At least, I thought we did."

"Ah yes," said Daddy. "Mummy wants a word with you two about why all her silver foil has been made into a useless silver carpet. And I'd like to know why my dressing gown keeps flapping open like a circus tent!"

Tom replied, "It's probably because your belt is lying in a dungeon in a puddle of slime."

"Tom," said Daddy. "I refuse to be the twit wearing a coat over his pyjamas. I want to wear a fully functioning dressing gown like a normal adult!"

The doorbell rang. Mummy answered it.

"Oh hello!" they heard her say. "How kind you are! Thank you, darling!"

Daddy galloped downstairs. "Come on! I've made you chicken soup and it's getting cold!"

"Was it a dream?" whispered Matt.

Tom sighed. "I suppose it must have been."

Tom, Matt and Baby slid sadly down the stairs without even saying 'wheeeee!'

Mummy smiled at them. "Isabella just knocked on the door. She said you left these at her house last time you visited. They're beautiful, but I don't remember them – were they from Grandma?"

Tom and Matt stared. Mummy was holding up two silver shimmery, shiny suits of armour – and a fireman's hose.

"NEE-NOR!" shouted Baby.

"One second," said Tom. "We forgot to wash our hands."

He and Matt scampered back upstairs, and ran into their bedroom, laughing and jumping.

TOM & MATT

Slowly, Tom pulled back Matt's duvet – and there, warm and cosy in the bed lay Tiny Dragon, with Mrs Dragon – both lovely squashy soft toys – and Daddy Dragon – who was a handsome, red, plastic dragon. They all had smiles on their dragon faces, and big crumbs of chocolate cake around their mouths.

The End